MW01025660

MEAN
WATERS

FRANK WOODSON

🎵 *Artesian* **Press**

P.O. Box 355 Buena Park, CA 90621

Take Ten Books
Adventure

Other Take Ten Themes:
Mystery
Sports
Disaster
Chillers
Thrillers
Fantasy

Project Editor:Liz Parker
Cover Illustrator:Marjorie Taylor
Cover Designer: Tony Amaro
Text Illustrator:Fujiko Miller
©2000 Artesian Press

ISBN 1-5869-015-4

Chapter 1

When Tom Addison was twelve years old he saved a grown man from drowning.

Tom wasn't really sure why he had done it. He didn't think he was brave. And he didn't think of himself as a hero after he did it. If he had thought anything at the time, it was maybe that he was a good swimmer, and the man wasn't. So he went in and helped him out. Simple as that.

The problem was that Tom had been afraid of the water ever since.

It had happened over four years before, and Tom, now sixteen, was still afraid. It embarrassed him. And it made him angry.

His best friend, Billy Thompson, who was a year older, had at first kidded him about it. It was on the local TV news, and Billy had called him the "local yokel hero." Or, "the muddy water rescue squad." Billy quit kidding about it when Tom offered to punch him one day.

"Just joking, Tom," Billy had said, "just joking."

It was a serious problem for Tom. He loved the rivers. He and Billy lived with the rivers. In boats on them, swimming in them, fishing, camping, and hunting along the banks. The rivers were their playgrounds.

"River rats," Tom's mother called them. "You boys always look like half-drowned rats. Why don't you find somethin' to do on dry land? The rivers worry me." But she didn't push it. She knew that they wouldn't listen.

There had been a big flood the year Tom had saved the man from drowning. But not as big as the one this year—some of the old people said this was the biggest flood they had ever seen.

Chapter 2

The low lands near the rivers flooded almost every year. Sometimes a little, sometimes a lot. Along with the four rivers were many lakes, ponds, and sloughs. In the floods they all became one big body of water. They were calm back-waters mostly, but near the rivers strong cross-currents could be dangerous. And there were whirlpools. Livestock, such as cows, pigs, and even horses, could be lost and drowned. So could people.

The year Tom was twelve and Billy was thirteen, the flood peaked during their spring break from school. The boys had spent their spare time during the winter building a boat. It was

Billy's idea, and they had worked on it in an old barn on his parent's property.

It was a flat-bottomed boat, modeled after the type most people used around there. They used old lumber of any size they could find. Across the middle they nailed two boards for seats. They filled all cracks and seams between the boards with caulking.

It was a rough-looking job. They built it of odds and ends found around Billy's place. Billy thought it was beautiful.

The boat was set up on two saw horses in the main part of the big barn. It was early Saturday morning before the spring break. Warm sunlight poured in on them.

Billy stood with his hands on his hips, a big grin on his face. "It's a beauty, isn't it, Tom? Just beautiful!"

Tom laughed. "Yeah. Not bad. Not bad. You think it'll actually float?"

"Sure it will! Of course it will! Look at that wood. Seasoned oak all around. Best kind of stuff, my dad said."

"Yeah," Tom said, "true. Speaking of your dad, you think he'll help us get it down to the water?"

Billy's face fell. "He's out of town. How about your dad? Could he carry the boat down in his pickup?"

Tom was uncertain. "I don't know.

He's been busy because of the flood. I'm not even sure if he's home. Let's go see."

Tom's dad was home, but he was busy with phone calls and paperwork. The boys waited over two hours before he could take them to the water.

He hauled the boys and their boat to a place just across the railroad tracks. A dirt farm road disappeared under floodwaters. "You boys be careful, you hear? Extra careful. Don't go anywhere near The Black. This boat wouldn't stand a chance! You hear me, Tom?" He looked hard at them. "Billy?"

"Yessir," said Tom.

"Nossir," said Billy.

Tom's dad laughed, shaking his head. "Okay, just keep to the still water. It'll float, I guess. If you'd told me you were building it, I could have helped. As soon as I get some time, I'll show you how to caulk it properly."

Mr. Addison climbed into the

pickup and drove off to town. He worked for the county water and power company. Flood problems kept him going night and day.

Chapter 3

By the time the boys had rowed the boat fifty feet from the road, they had two inches of water in the bottom of the boat. Billy sat with a paddle, working hard to keep the boat moving straight. Tom sat in the middle, working just as hard with an old coffee can, bailing the water out.

"We're gonna sink," Tom yelled, but he was laughing.

Billy laughed too. "So what? You can swim. Besides, it's not gonna sink. It's a good boat." He paddled harder, looking into the bottom of the boat. "Your dad's right, though, we didn't get the caulking right."

Tom grunted, scooping up water.

They were soon soaked with cold water to the knees, but they hardly noticed. They laughed and joked.

Upriver about a mile they came into a section where young trees and bushes stuck up through the water. They took the boat into the area.

With the easing of the rains the weather had become warm and soft. It was the kind of weather that brought people out into the sun. And other creatures. Like snakes.

The boys were well into the trees when Tom spotted the first one. He quit bailing. "Hey, Billy, look at that. Little critter's getting some sun."

Billy stopped paddling. "What? Look at what?"

"Over there." Tom nodded to the front and left. "Snake. A water moccasin. In that little tree."

The snake was coiled in the fork of a small tree about five feet from the front of the boat. It was brown, about

three feet long. Slender and fast looking. Its head was up and pointed at
them.

"Snake! Ah, nooo!" Billy started
back paddling, trying to pull the boat
around. "Let's get into some open water!"

Billy hated snakes. Snakes were about the only thing Tom knew of that could scare his friend. Tom was not afraid of them. But he tried to give them plenty of room.

As Billy brought the boat around Tom looked back at the trees and bushes they had come through. "Uh-oh," he said, "looks like we got ourselves into a little snake patch, Billy."

Billy stopped paddling again. Every tree and bush seemed to have one or two snakes in it. They were coiled in forks, or stretched along branches. They must have been there when the boys came through. They had been too busy to notice.

Billy was a big boy with good muscles, quick hands, and a laughing way of dealing with most things. Now he wasn't laughing. His usually high-energy, red face was pale. "We can't go back through there, Tom." His voice was low and tight.

Tom looked in the other direction. "If we go out that way we'll be close to the current of The Black."

"I don't care," said Billy, "I'd rather fight The Black than go back through them snakes." He put the paddle into the water hard, bringing the boat about. There were only a few trees between them and open water.

They were soon clear of the trees and bushes, except for one large thicket ahead and a little upriver. This patch of bushes, the boys knew, grew near the bank of The Black. Although they were still a hundred yards from the big river, they could already feel the tug of the current.

"I'm going to head downstream," Billy said. "We can cut back toward shore when we get past the snake patch."

"The Black bends in down that way," Tom said. "The current's pretty strong along there."

"We can handle it." Billy's voice was still tight.

Then they saw the man.

Chapter 4

He was a big man in a boat much like theirs. The boat emerged from behind the trees near the banks of The Black. The boat was not in the strongest current, but it was near. And it was moving fast. The man was trying to control it with a pole.

When he saw the boys he yelled something.

"What did he say?" Billy was working hard, turning the boat downstream.

"I'm not sure," Tom said. "Something about cows."

The man waved, then pulled the pole into the boat, standing up. He cupped one hand around his mouth. "You boys seen any cows along here?

Two of them?"

"Lord!" Billy said, "he's either crazy or doesn't know anything about boats."

For a moment it was funny to Tom. He laughed and yelled, "Nossir. Just some snakes. You better watch it. That current will…"

But it was too late. The man's boat started turning sideways in the current. Then it hit the full force of the current. The boat came to a stop for an instant. The big man lost his balance, yelled something, then went over the side. He disappeared under muddy, swirling water.

Tom sat stunned for a moment.

"Bail, Tom, bail! We gotta get to him. He can't swim."

Tom came to life. "What?"

"He can't swim. Didn't you hear him? We gotta get out there."

The man's boat, free of his weight, spun about and was sucked off downstream like a leaf. Then the pole popped to the surface. And then the man. He let out a gurgling yell, "Help!" He started splashing the water with his arms and twisting about. Total panic.

Tom was on his knees at the front of the boat. He looked at the man, looked over his shoulder at Billy. Then he looked at the three or four inches of water in the bottom of the boat.

Tom jerked his t-shirt over his head. Rolling around, he untied his shoes with fast fingers. Kicking them off, he stood up.

"Tom, what are you gonna do? That current is mean. He's too big for you...!"

Tom said, "Catch up, Billy." And he shot forward in a dive.

Tom was a tall, slender boy, not as big as Billy, but strong for his size. And he was about the best swimmer in the county. Within seconds he was pulling close to the struggling man.

"Relax," he yelled. "Just relax."

But the man kept flapping his arms and twisting in a circle. His face was red and scared, his eyes wild. "Help," his voice trembled, "I'm—I'm sorry—I can't—can't swim."

The man twisted around again and started to slip under. Tom darted forward, reaching to get a hold of his shirt. But the man came back up, saw Tom, and grabbed him.

A big hand gripped Tom's upper arm. Then the man had him around the waist. They both went under. The drowning man had Tom in a death hold.

It was then that Tom's fear of the water began.

Chapter 5

Tom fought to get free, squirming and pushing. Black, gritty water pulled them down. Tom got his elbows into the man's stomach, pushing with all his strength. But the big farmer was far stronger. Wild fear rushed through Tom. He started kicking and trying to punch the monster that was killing him.

The man suddenly let go of Tom's waist and grabbed his shoulders. He kicked upward, pushing Tom down. One big shoe caught Tom on the forehead. But he was free!

Tom shot down into cold, cold water. Then he reversed and went up, fighting to hold his breath a little longer. Fighting to control his panic.

When he broke the surface, Tom's arms kept working, as if he would lift himself into the air. He gasped in air, then breathed more carefully. Again.

"Tom!" He heard Billy as if from far away. "Tommy! You all right? I'm comin' as fast as I can!"

Tom saw him through a haze of water and fear. Still many yards away, paddling like a crazy person.

The man was a few feet from him. Still away from the crosscurrents. Otherwise The Black would already have him. His arms beat weakly. His head was barely above water.

Tom kept away from him. He dog-paddled in place.

The man was wearing bib overalls. Two straps crossed on his back. Tom waited. When the man's strength was about gone, Tom swam closer. He stayed behind the man. When the man was about to go under, Tom grabbed the straps. He started kicking backwards.

Tom kicked and kicked and kicked. He kicked until his feet and legs were too tired to move ever again. If he ever got to stop.

Kicking and kicking. He heard Billy yelling, "Tom! I got you. It's okay. Hang onto the boat. We'll make it!"

Finally they hit shallow water. The big farmer was able to touch bottom. He helped push the boat.

Some men and boys near the railroad tracks had seen them. Three of the men waded in to help.

They reached dry ground a mile downriver from the dirt farm road.

There was a buzz of excitement when Billy told what had happened. Everybody wanted to talk to Tom. But he would not talk. When he got the chance, he slipped away.

When they did the TV news story, Tom still would not talk. The story was only a few seconds long. There was a clip of the town and the muddy river. Because of Tom's silence, everybody let it die quickly.

After that, if Tom saw the farmer in town, he would take a different direction. He noticed that if the man saw him first, he did the same.

Four years later they were both still

embarrassed by their fear.

Chapter 6

Now the whole county seemed to be flooded. The water had crossed the railroad and was into the lower streets. The school year had ended two weeks early because of the flooding. Farming and business stopped almost completely.

"What do you think, Tom?" Billy said. "We can just take it up along the tracks there. Keep away from currents." He grinned. "And snakes."

Tom didn't answer at first. He was looking out across miles of water.

The boys were standing on a rocky bluff north of town. Just below them ran the railroad tracks. The tracks were just visible through the water.

"I don't know, Billy. I may have to work." For the past two summers Tom had helped his uncle in his Texaco station across the river.

Billy snorted. "Nah! Nobody can drive anywhere. Just like my dad's business. We can't make any deliveries." He hesitated. "Uh, Tom, I know you don't much like boats, and, uh, water, anymore. But you'd like my new boat. It's a beauty!"

Billy had also worked the past two summers. His father operated an oil company. He sold and delivered motor oil and fuel oil to farmers. Billy helped in the equipment yards. He would also go along with his father on deliveries.

The summer work had helped Tom avoid going to the rivers with his friend. It helped him avoid showing his fear.

"My dad will let me use the company pickup," Billy said. "We can put the boat in upriver a ways. There's nobody around up there. I've only had it out once. It handles really great, Tom!" He laughed. "Better than that one we built."

Tom turned red, feeling angry. But he knew his friend wasn't making fun of him. The anger helped him decide. "Okay, let's do it!"

An hour later they were out on the water. Tom sat in the middle seat. He looked straight ahead.

The boat was a canoe. Sleek and fast. It was dark blue with white stripes.

Billy's strong paddle strokes sent the canoe skimming over the quiet water. "It's something, isn't it, Tom? It's big enough to carry four or five people, but light as a feather."

Tom glanced over his shoulder and nodded. He turned back to the front. He tried not to look at the water. If he did, he saw black, gritty water, swirling around him. He felt the heavy arms around his waist.

Fighting his thoughts, Tom lost track of the moment. Suddenly he realized that the canoe was still. He turned around carefully, looking at Billy.

Billy sat looking at Tom. His face was serious. He kept the canoe in place with a gentle back and forth paddle stroke.

"What's going on, Billy? See some snakes?" Tom smiled.

Billy shook his head. He smiled a little, too. "Nah. Uh, Tom...? Do you remember that guy you pulled out of The Black?"

The fear Tom had been trying to put down trembled up through his whole body. "Of course I do! How could I forget something like that?" Anger at his friend mixed with the fear. "Why are you bringing that up?"

"Did you ever get to know him?" Billy's whole body was stiff now. He leaned forward.

Tom glared at him. Shook his head.

"I did," Billy said. "He's really nice. He has a farm up across The Black." Billy was talking fast now. "He has three kids. A brand new three-month-old baby girl, an older girl of about fifteen, I think, and a boy about five. His name's Ray Kincaid. His wife's a nice lady. They have a farm, but, you know, it's in that corner of the county surrounded by three rivers. It's not good in a flood like this."

Billy suddenly quit talking. He looked away from Tom.

Tom let go of his fear long enough to look hard at his friend. "What is it, Billy?"

Billy looked back. "I'm very worried, Tom. Mary Ellen and I talk on the phone about every day. And I ..."

"Who's Mary Ellen?"

"Ray's daughter. We ..."

"Is she your girlfriend?"

"Sort of, yes. I guess. But, the thing

is ..."

Tom jumped in again. "Did you get to know them because of ... because of **me and** what happened?" Tom swung his legs around and sat facing Billy. "Have you been talking to them about me, Billy?"

Billy was completely surprised. The anger and hurt were clear on Tom's face. "*No!* What do you mean? I wouldn't do that. My dad and I take oil and fuel out to them. Dad's been taking me along for the last year and a half." Billy stopped, then said softly, "I wouldn't talk about you, Tom. Not the way you mean. You're my friend."

Tom glared at him for a moment. Then he looked down. The anger bled away. "Okay," he mumbled. "What has you worried?"

"I'm afraid they're cut off up there, Tom. Their phone has been out for three days. The bridge across Current River is down. They can't get in or out that way. That's the way Dad and I always go. The road north out of their place is low. It may have flooded too deeply to use. And ... well ... I gotta do something!"

It was quiet for a moment. Then Tom looked at Billy. "And ...?" he said. "What do you want to do, Billy?"

Billy leaned forward. "I want us to take this canoe upstream. Cross over The Black above Fisher Bend, and get to their place. We can paddle right up to their farmhouse. We can do it—this is a good boat! I want you to go with me. But if you won't, you won't. I'll have to try it by myself."

Tom's mind shut down on his fear. Fear locked itself in the middle of his stomach.

"Why didn't you say so? Let's get going."

Billy laughed. "All right! Grab that spare paddle, Tommy." He dug in the water with the paddle.

Tom unhooked the spare paddle from the inside of the boat. He got onto his knees for more power. He, too, dug in. The light canoe shot across the muddy back-waters.

Chapter 7

Usually The Black could be crossed in about ten minutes. It took the boys almost an hour of heavy going to make it. And they hit calm waters over a mile downriver from where they wanted to be.

They were both soaked. An inch of water covered the bottom of the canoe. Their arms felt as heavy as lead.

"Some boat, huh?" Billy gasped.

"Yeah," said Tom. "Some river."

Billy grunted. "Mean sucker."

"How far is the farm?"

"About a mile and a half in. Up across Jane's Creek. Are you up to it?"

"Yeah."

They sent the canoe scooting across

the waters.

They crossed Jane's Creek. Inland the ground rose. In a short time Tom could see trees. Within the trees was a flash of white.

"There it is!" Billy said. "Back through that bunch of trees."

They were able to bring the boat through the trees. The flood waters rose to within a hundred yards of the Kincaid farmhouse. Beyond the house stood a barn. The white split-level house was two stories tall at one end. The garage sat on lower ground, dangerously close to Jane's Creek. The other end of the house sat on higher ground. Jane's Creek cut a deep ditch a hundred feet to the north of the buildings.

Beyond the buildings the boys could see more floodwaters. Water surrounded the area.

They brought the boat onto wet ground. A light sprinkling of rain had begun.

They climbed stiffly from the boat. Billy tied it to the trunk of a tall, slender oak tree. They started toward the house.

There was a John Deere tractor and a big trailer pulled up to the front porch. They could see household goods loaded in the trailer.

A big man came out of the front door. He carried a heavy box across the porch. Behind him came a teenage girl. She carried an armload of clothing.

"Hey," Billy shouted. "Hello." He waved.

The man and girl stopped.

Billy trotted forward, and Tom followed.

The girl's face broke into a confused smile.

The big man grinned. "Hey, Billy! Good Lord. Where'd you come from?" He went down the porch steps and lifted the box into the back of the trailer. The girl did the same with the clothing.

"Hi, Mary Ellen," Billy said as they came up.

"Hello, Billy." Long brown hair fell about her shoulders. Blue eyes grinned at Billy from her pretty face.

As soon as Tom saw the man, the fear at his center began to spread.

The big farmer looked at Tom. "Hello, Tom." His voice was quiet. His green eyes looked at Tom.

Tom nodded and looked away.

"Hello, Tom," Mary Ellen said.

Tom glanced sharply at her, then looked away.

A little boy ran out onto the porch. A puppy trotted behind him. "Billy!" he yelled. "How did you get here, Dude?"

Billy laughed. "Hi, Timmy. Magic, of course. What did you think? *Dude.*"

"How *did* you boys get here?" Ray Kincaid asked.

"Across The Black."

Kincaid stared at him. "Why?"

Billy shrugged. "We ... uh ... thought you might need some help."

Ray Kincaid didn't say anything. He just reached up and squeezed Billy's shoulder. "Okay. Good. Well, we have to get out of here. Our power is out. The phones are out. And we got a report that Foshee River might flood. If that happens, we're going to get some mean waters down on this farm."

Ray Kincaid turned and started up the steps. "We have a few more things to load, then we're heading out."

Billy and the others followed.

"Where's Mrs. Kincaid? And the baby?" He asked.

"I sent them over to her cousin's house in Peach Grove." He paused inside the living room, looking at Tom. "We got all the livestock out a week ago. I didn't want to take any chances."

"Is that tractor high enough to pull you out of here?" Billy asked.

"I hope so," said Kincaid. "Liz took the pickup. I followed her with the tractor. That was two days ago. The truck just barely made it."

"Foshee's nothing but a mud stream!" Tom suddenly blurted. "Slow as a turtle. Do they think it'll really break out?"

Kincaid shrugged. "I don't know. Anything can happen with this kind of water."

Chapter 8

"Dad!" Timmy's small voice came from the porch. "Come look. Something's going on." He sounded both excited and afraid.

They all headed for the front porch.

Timmy stood looking north across the water toward Peach Grove. Across what was normally a corn field there was water. All along the edge of the woods it looked like the water was boiling black.

"What in the world?" Ray Kincaid's voice was filled with awe.

The black boiling water was laced with white.

"It broke!" Billy shouted. "Foshee flooded!"

The water was pouring out from the woods now. It was at least six feet high, all across the field, moving fast.

"Inside," Kincaid yelled. "Get upstairs." He bent and swept Timmy up in one big arm.

They crossed the living room and pounded up the stairs.

Timmy screamed, "Where's Vom?"

Kincaid stopped and looked around. "Where *is* that mutt?"

But it was too late.

The wall of water hit the north side of the house. It felt like they had been rammed by a big truck with a rubber nose. The house shook, groaned, trembled. That side of the house seemed to sag.

A rush of dirty water, two feet deep, swirled into the driveway. They heard the terrified barks of the little dog.

"Vom!" Timmy screamed.

Kincaid crowded them upstairs and

to the side of the house that stood on higher ground. Billy and Tom ran into a bedroom and to a window. The water split around the side of the house. It hit it with heavy hammer blows. It swirled and sucked at the base of the house. The house creaked and groaned. To Tom, it felt like it was moving. But he wasn't sure.

Another burst of water came, smaller than the first. Then another smaller one. The water poured across the land, heading for lower ground. It headed for the swollen Black.

The house held.

Within a short time only an inch or two of water remained in the yard. But Jane's Creek was still rising fast.

"God!" Billy mumbled, "that's the worst I've *ever* seen."

Suddenly Mary Ellen let out a scream. "Timmy! Where's Timmy?"

Kincaid and the boys whirled around. "Timmy! Tim!" The big farmer moved fast for his size. But Billy was the fastest.

Billy went down the stairs four and five at a time. By the time the others hit the front porch, Billy was dashing toward Jane's Creek.

Timmy was ahead of him. An old apple tree grew near the creek's edge. It was thick with branches, leaves, and green apples. Timmy was climbing it.

A third of the way up in the tree was Vom. He was caught in a thick nest of small twigs and branches. The water had picked him up and tossed him into the tree. He shivered and whimpered as Timmy climbed.

Jane's Creek roared like an express train. The water was thirty feet across. Foshee River was sending its waters down the creek. It was pulling anything it could get hold of along with it, including the river banks. The ground around the apple tree was being eaten away.

"Timmy. Hold on," Billy yelled. "I'll get Vom!"

But the boy had already squirmed into the tree. He had the puppy in his arms.

Billy went up after him as quick as a cat. "Here, give me the puppy. Hurry!"

The others ran up.

"Get back," Billy called. "This ground is going to go. *Timmy!* Give Vom to me."

The boy struggled around, held the puppy out with both hands. Billy took him in one arm. He was holding onto a branch with his other hand. His feet braced against the thick bark. He lowered the dog, and Ray Kincaid grabbed it, giving it quickly to Mary Ellen.

Billy scrambled higher into the tree. "Here, Tim, lean out. I'll get you." He got the boy under the armpits.

Just then a huge hunk of earth gave way next to the tree. The tree started to lean toward Jane's Creek.

Billy turned, letting Tim's arms slip through his hands. He held him at the wrists and swung him back.

"Mr. Kincaid. Catch!" He swung Timmy forward and let him go.

Ray Kincaid caught his son in his big, strong arms.

"Billy," Tom cried, "get out of there!"

Chapter 9

Just as Billy moved to drop from the tree, the tree toppled. More ground fell away. The tree twisted. Billy was caught in the branches.

The tree and Billy went into the roaring creek.

"Billy!" Mary Ellen screamed. She started forward.

Her father grabbed her with one hand. "Get back! Get back! The whole bank is going."

They scrambled back as more dirt was sucked away. Water boiled into the gap where the tree had been.

The apple tree rolled in the current. Billy went under, then came up. He struggled to get free.

Ray Kincaid moved back. He pulled the sobbing Mary Ellen with him. Tom stood, stunned.

"Tom, get back. That bank's not safe." Kincaid's voice seemed to come from far off.

The old apple tree was twisted and bent. The mean waters couldn't seem to get a hold of it. The tree spun in a circle. Billy clung to the branches.

On the far bank, about two hundred feet down, was more solid ground. A big oak tree grew there. Its big roots reached into the flooded creek.

The apple tree spun in a heavy circle toward the oak. It rolled again, and Billy disappeared. When he came up again he was out of the branches. He clutched the twisted trunk with both arms.

"He might make it," Tom shouted, "if he can get to that oak!"

As the apple tree went near the oak, a fierce current grabbed it. The tree was spun like a top. Its branches hit the bank. The trunk swung around and was slammed into the roots of the oak. Billy was caught between the trunk and a big root.

The apple tree was stuck there.

Billy's head and upper chest were out of water. One arm was flung across

the trunk of the apple tree. But it was lifeless.

"He's dead," Mary Ellen cried, "Daddy, he's dead!"

Timmy and the puppy were whimpering.

"Maybe not," Kincaid said. He set Timmy down. "Get back, son. Go to the house." The boy took Vom from his sister and moved a few feet back.

"Maybe he's just knocked out," Kincaid continued. "We have to get him out of there. That tree can break loose anytime."

He turned to his daughter. "Mary Ellen, get me that rope off the back porch. The water won't have gotten to it. Go, girl, hurry!"

Mary Ellen ran.

Turning to Tom, Kincaid said, "The rope's long enough to reach. We can tie it around your waist. You can get to Billy. I'll give you plenty of rope. You can get hold of Billy. Get around his waist from behind. Then you can just let the current and the rope swing you back across. I can handle your weight."

Kincaid's words were calm, even, clear. But it took a long minute for Tom to understand them. When he did, he started to tremble.

"I … I can't."

Kincaid turned and shouted. "Mary Ellen, hurry!" He turned back to Tom. "I can hold you, Tom. If the current takes you too far, I'll swing you back to shore." He hesitated. "We have to try, Tommy. Or Billy will be gone."

Tom couldn't look at him. It was raining harder now. Part of the wetness on Tom's face was tears.

"I … I'm afraid. I haven't been in the water since … since …"

Kincaid grabbed Tom's shoulders. "Tom, listen. I know. Billy has told me some of it. But you have to understand. That river didn't try to drown you. And you didn't try to drown yourself.

Billy said you're as good as an Olympic swimmer. *I* tried to drown you, to save myself. I'm ashamed of it, but it's the truth."

Chapter 10

Tom looked into Kincaid's broad face and green eyes. For a moment his mind was blank. Then he said, "How come you never learned to swim?"

Kincaid suddenly smiled. "I'm from Kansas. Up there we pray for the rain to start. Down here, we pray for it to stop." He squeezed Tom's shoulders. "Look, Tommy, I can't swim. But I'm strong, and I'm good with a rope. I owe my life to you. And now I owe Billy, too. I won't lose you. And we *can* save Billy." He looked hard into Tom's eyes. "Ready?"

Tom sniffled and shrugged.

Mary Ellen came puffing up with a big coil of rope.

Then it was happening, and Tom didn't know if he was afraid or not. He pulled his t-shirt and shoes off. Kincaid tied the rope around his waist.

Tom stood for an instant and took a breath. Then he ran a few steps and dived. A long, clean dive. Kincaid played the rope out just right.

Tom hit and skimmed on the water for a few feet. He worked the water like a water bug. Then the water got to him. But he fought it. He stroked like he'd never stroked in his life. Confident. Strong. *Mean waters?* He was meaner!

But he almost missed.

The current tumbled and rolled him like a cork. He was shooting past Billy and the apple tree. With a final effort, he grabbed and got a hold of a root. He hung on. It felt like his arm was being pulled from his shoulder. But he hung on.

Tom worked his way toward Billy

and reached under the trunk. Then he had a grip on Billy's belt and waistband.

Tom stopped, resting for an instant. How would he get Billy free? The current ripped at him. He saw Billy's white face. Blood oozed from a cut on his head.

It took Tom a moment to realize the apple tree was moving. It was being pulled out from the oak.

Still gripping Billy's belt, Tom went under. He fought desperately to pull Billy deep, to get him free of the moving tree. He felt the branches scraping across his back. And then they· were rolling and tumbling in the current again. His hand was locked on Billy's belt. He would never let go. Then another tree was near him, pulling at his hair.

His lungs were bursting. He could hold it no longer. Now he would drown. He opened his mouth. But instead of black, gritty water pouring into his lungs, a great gasp of air poured in.

He coughed and sputtered.

"Hold on, Tommy! Daddy's coming."

Mary Ellen knelt on the stormy bank. She had a handful of his hair in one hand, a handful of Billy's in the other. She strained to keep their heads out of water.

Then Kincaid was there. His big farmer's hands pulled them out.

They collapsed on solid ground.

Billy had swallowed water. And he had a bad cut on his head. But within half an hour he had come around. He would be okay. He lay on the ground with a weak grin on his face.

"What do you think, Tom?" Mary Ellen said, "I mean about...?"

"You mean about swimming and water?" Tom finished for her. "I don't know. Coach Anderson asked me to get on his swimming team a couple of years ago. He said I might make state competition. Or even national. I think I'll do that." He grinned.

Billy laughed. "The way this flood looks, everybody in the state better try to get on that team."